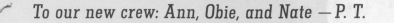

To our new crew: Ann, Obie, and Nate — P. T.

For Jenna — J.

PICK A PUMPKIN

Patricia Toht   illustrated by Jarvis

CANDLEWICK PRESS

Pick a pumpkin
from the patch—

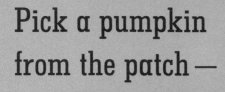

tall and lean
or short and fat.

Vivid orange,
ghostly white,
or speckled green
might be just right.

PICK ME

PUMPKINS
FOR
SALE

PICK ME

Pumpkin snugly
in your arms,
wheel a wagon
through the farm.

Stop for mugs
of spicy punch,
toffee apples,
sweet to crunch.

Homeward from
the pumpkin patch,
all your goodies
stacked in back.

Now . . .

brush or wipe your pumpkin clean.
Rub it smooth and make it gleam.

Find the perfect carving space,
lined with papers just in case
you make a mess.

Next . . .

gather other
things you need:
a bowl, a spoon
for scooping seeds,

FLOUR

BUG
JUICE

a tool to trace
a spooky face,
and plastic saws
for cutting shapes.

Then . . .

invite around
a friend or two—

form a
PUMPKIN-
CARVING
CREW!

Let grown-ups cut the top a bit,
big enough for hands to fit.
Reach down deep into the hole,
grab the seeds, and give a pull.

Lumpy chunks. Sticky strings.
Clumpy seeds. Guts and things.
With a spoon, scrape sides neatly.
Clean the inside out completely.

Now all together . . .

carve the eyes.

Giant circles of surprise.

Small slits sleeping

or one eye peeping.

Cross-eyed crazy.

Angry. Lazy.

And below those . . .

make a nose.
A triangle. A pinprick.
A nose that grows
from thin to thick.

Under the nose . . .

Before you light your new creation,
first it's time for decorations!

Cobwebs strung from post to post.
Rings of gauzy dancing ghosts.
Spiders. Tombstones.
Dangling bats.
Skeletons and witches' hats.

Now quick!
Slip on gear
to trick-or-treat
and grab a sack
to hold your sweets.

Lift your pumpkin up with pride.
March it to a place outside.
Set it safely on the ground,
and call the crew
      to gather round.

Ask someone to strike a match.
Watch! The candle's wick
will catch.

See it glow outside your door.

LOOK!
It's not a pumpkin
anymore.

It's a . . .

JACK-O'-LANTERN!

Its red-hot eyes
will gaze
and flicker.

Its fiery grin
will blaze and snicker,
to guard your house
while you have fun.

Happy Halloween,

everyone!